The End

The Final Chapter of Humanity

ISHA TAHA

Table of Contents

<u>Introduction</u>

In the beginning, God created the earth knowing that one day he would destroy it. The way that he knew Adam would eat from the tree of knowledge. God told us there would be warning signs. If we watch for them, we will have a better idea of when Jesus will return to earth to bring his people to heaven. First, little things began to happen, things that most people didn't pay much attention to. But as soon as bad things start happening close to home people begin to open their eyes. They begin to pray and ask questions. They begin to prepare themselves for the worst, but by then it was already too late. God speaks of these many warning signs in his book The Holy Bible. Often time people pray more than they read which is why many of the warning signs were overlooked. I am unable to recall the years in which these events took place, but I can tell you about the order in which these events began to happen.

Natural disasters are a sign that things would be coming to an end. The couple of events that stood out in my mind were Hurricane Katrina in Louisiana, and the big earthquake over in Haiti. Haiti's disaster happened in 2010. Everyone reached out to help those people in their time of need. Many people died and too many of them were injured. These events were so easily overlooked as warning signs by the one's who's hearts were not really following God.

Then sometime later the beast came with its special mark. The mark was to be worn only by his soldiers. If you were not following the anti-Christ, then you were against him. There was no choice of being in between. Those who were against him many of them were killed. There were a lot of people who decided to follow the anti-Christ. The remaining followers of God would have to survive on earth until Jesus would return in the end. My name is Isha, and this is where my story begins. I was one of the remaining survivors. I can't tell you all of the events that happened at the beginning of the end of the world, only the things that impacted me

the most. I can tell you about the feelings that
I had, the nightmares too, and all that God
had done to help me make it through.

Chapter 1

Learning the Truth

If it is the truth, we seek.

I know we shall find.

If it is understanding, we wish to know.

Only God will open our mind.

As I awoke one Saturday morning, in almost a dreamlike state of mind. I was unable to remember what had happened to me the night before. I began looking around the room in an unfamiliar place that didn't feel like home to me. Sitting up from the hardwood floor with a small brown blanket wrapped around me. I sat up and took a quick look around. It was a small house, and very much an older home. The house had wood paneling walls throughout. The home reminded me of one of those log cabin homes that could have been used as vacation spot or a personal getaway place. It was mildly cool in the house.

 I looked out of the window, not far from where I was lying, and could see an oak tree standing tall and full of many green leaves. Just then, in the distance, I could hear a few men talking. I couldn't see their faces because the trees were blocking my view. When they got closer to the house, I could only see the tops of their heads as they passed by the window. I couldn't make out what they were saying, but I could hear them laughing.

Just then, the door makes a loud creak, and three men enter the house.

"She's up," says one of the gentlemen with long hair. "We were getting worried about you Isha since you fell and bumped your head on that rock yesterday. Wasn't sure that you would be okay, but we are glad to see that you are up now."

"Are you hungry," asked another gentleman with a big smile. "We found an apple tree just up the hill. Can you believe that?"

"And Johnathan managed to get a couple of fish from the lake, but there won't be much more to eat after today so we must keep moving," said the first gentleman with the long hair.

I meekly nodded my head yes.

"You are definitely not as talkative as you normally are," said the long-haired guy. Are you sure you are all right?"

"I'm fine."

"I know you still need to rest, so don't let us disturb you."

Sitting there thinking while trying to collect my thoughts I said to myself, I don't remember hitting my head yesterday! I don't recall any of that. I must have amnesia. I do remember my name being Isha and where I was born. I also have memories of my brother graduating from college. I remembered how my aunt would through my cousin and I birthday parties together since we shared the same birthday. I just can't figure out why I don't remember yesterday. That is just too hard to believe. Who were these three guys that were of no relation to me? They didn't seem very harmful, but quite friendly, but why was I with them?

So many thoughts began to run through my mind, but none of them made much sense. I thought maybe we were on some kind of church mission trip, but if that was the case then where are the people that we are helping? I thought about the fact that we were looking for food, so maybe we are on some survival show. I knew that couldn't be the case because I vowed never to be on one of those shows. Besides, where were the cameras? Too much to figure out on my own, so I told the men what happened to me, and they began to help me be able to regain some of my memory back.

Johnathan and Jeremy were brothers, but that wasn't too hard to figure out because their facial features were remarkably similar. Johnathan leads our little group. He has a very calm demeanor and seems to have a lot of wisdom for his age. Although I never asked him his age, I would guess he was in his mid-forties. Johnathan had short brown hair, brown eyes and was about 6'1" in height. He stood tall, proud, and eager to serve God. He came across to me like a father figure, and he didn't seem to talk much. It was like he had to keep his mind constantly focused. He was the glue that kept the group together.

His brother Jeremy on the other hand was the complete opposite. Jeremy was a funny guy who was always there to make you smile. He had long brown hair with green eyes, and he stood about the same height as his brother. Jeremy had a more muscular build with a soft mustache on his face. Both brothers were Caucasian, but Jeremy had more of a tan than his brother. Jeremy seemed to make the best of life even when it gets tough. He liked wearing flannel shirts and tight blue jeans. Jeremy dressed more like a farm boy without boots. I was at least brave enough to ask him how old he was since he was more laid back than his brother. Jeremy was 35. He had never been married and didn't have any children of his own, and so he was extremely close to his older brother.

Michael was the youngest of the three men and the shyest. At the age of 32 and a height of 5'9" Michael stood out to be a strong-willed man. He was tan with long black hair and deep brown eyes that you could gaze at all day. Michael was a Native American who spoke about three different languages other than his own native tongue. He spoke English, Arabic, and German. Michael had served in the military where he had spent most of his time in Germany and Saudi Arabia. I must admit he was quite a handsome man with his baby face skin. He also had a very muscular figure. Michael was fond of me. He liked my brown skin, small figure, and the fact that I was the youngest in the group. I was only 28 and about 130lbs, but I felt like I could keep up with them.

After speaking with them for a while, the best thing I could figure out was that somehow, I managed to block out all the terrible things that had been going on in the world over the last couple of weeks.

First, there was an unexpected hurricane that hit Florida. Then another terrorist attack in DC that killed 2,000 people and over 1,000 injured parties from a car bomb that was set off in a couple of tourist attraction locations. It came close to the White House but everyone there was okay. Then there was a huge oil spill that ruined a lot of crops for the U.S. this year.

It was getting crazy out there. Not really knowing who to trust or which way to go next, I knew that we had to keep our faith in God. I just remember thinking to myself that no matter what was going on in the world today, that God had placed me with these men for a reason. I had no reason to question God's plans, but I was so glad to know that I wasn't alone in the world. I felt safe enough not to worry about them harming me. After being up for an hour or so I went back and rested.

As the day began to quickly go by, it was getting extremely dark outside. We had just sat down to eat our last meal for the night.

"Thank you for the food," I politely said to Johnathan.

"You're very welcome," he replied.

"So how are you feeling," asked Michael.

"Much better," I said. "How did we all meet?" I asked, trying so desperately to recall something from my past. Jeremy immediately began to talk.

"Well, it all began when we all had to stand in front of this army. Satan's army is what I called it. Two soldiers would come down the line from each end and ask each person if they were going to take the mark of the beast. The other soldiers stood in a row across from the people with guns loaded and ready to use on anyone if they dare try to run. We were all scared, but no one ran. A couple began to pray, and I know in my mind I did also. Some people passed out, but the soldiers would come around and stand them back on their feet if they did. One older man in fact died of a heart attack. Some say he got off easy, but I don't know about that. I don't consider any pain to be an easy death, but that's just me."

As he kept talking, I slowly began to remember bits and pieces of everything as little flashbacks in my head, but still most of it was pretty fuzzy. I couldn't even imagine what would happen next. Jeremy continued.

"They had everyone stand in front of the soldiers in groups of fifty people at a time. In some of the groups prior to ours, there were people that had decided to take the mark and walk in the path of darkness. Our group of fifty on the other hand had all decided to be God's followers. No one decided to take the mark of the beast, and this made their leader extremely angry, and that's when it happened. The soldiers took their place, said some kind of prayer to their god and then began to fire. The soldiers were already instructed as to which people were to be killed and which ones to keep alive. As they fired, we stood there and watched all of our family die right in front of us; leaving just 10 people of the 50 left to tell the story to anyone who would decide to cross him."

"I still say it was fate," replied Michael. "God's will that we ten of many were saved."

Johnathan and Jeremy agreed.

I started to rub my head because I could feel a massive headache beginning to form all over my head. I had visualized what they were saying, and it was like I was reliving it all over again. I can't even describe how it felt. I was angry, upset, and most of all incredibly sad. This event just brings me closer to God because anyone that would do such horrible things could never convince me to serve them. My God is a loving God, not a monster. How could anyone be this way? I know it happened because it was written in God's plan. I know it's not my job to question God, so I won't. His will be done. Since God had chosen to save me, it had become my mission to make sure that I did my best to honor him. I will follow him until he brings my life to an end.

"It was hard for us to deal with the loss of our loved ones," says Johnathan. "My brother and I lost our mother, my wife and Jeremy's wife to be. Michael lost his wife and his daughter. And Isha you lost your mom, brother, and unborn child. Your husband had passed away prior to these events from a car accident."

Johnathan continued with the story. "After they finished killing our families, they beat us beyond recognition. We bled from head to toe, with cuts from our forehead to our feet. It was as if they had wanted us to bleed to death. Then they threw us out into the streets like food for the fowls of the air to come and eat us. It took us four hours to get up enough strength to get up and try to move to a safe location. Just at that time a few other people came to help us. They came for us as God had instructed them. One by one they began taking us from the street and into their home. They took you first since you were bleeding more than some of the others. They cleaned us up and nurtured us back into good health. If my memory is correct there were six of them that came from the house to help us. One man was a doctor, and one of the women was a nurse.

"Michael kept a special eye out for you," winked Jeremy. "You reminded him of his wife. She was very loving and beautiful from what he told me. Michael would come over and check on you often to see if you would be okay since you had lost your child."

"Well, thank you all for all that you have done for me," I replied. "I am truly grateful."

"No problem," replied Jeremy. "Just make sure you return the favor," laughed Jeremy.

"So, whatever happened to the rest of the surviving ten?"

"Two of them that happened to be a married couple decided to open another shelter for people to go to when they had left the devils' army camp," said Johnathan. "But the other four were later killed by not having the will to survive. They became weak in the heart and weak in the mind. They had allowed things to bother them instead of giving their pain to God. It became too much for them to bear, because they tried to carry the load on their own backs instead of God's and they eventually just gave up."

Chapter 2

<u>Many Days of Traveling</u>

We must travel to find.
What it is that we seek.
We must look hard.
We cannot linger.
We must be meek.
As we lift-up our heads
Following the signs of our Lord
We know it will be hard.
So, we must carry our own sword.
Pray for us along the way.
We need guidance.
We need strength.
To make it another day
Call the angels.
Call them all.
Let them lift us up.
So that we cannot fall

During our journey we came upon a group of people that did not have the mark of the beast,

"Hey, how are you guys?" replied one of the strangers.

"Fine," Johnathan replied.

"We are surprised to see you 4 out here," said the stranger.

"We have been out here for a while and haven't seen anyone come pass. My name is Timothy," and this is Vincent and Charles."

"My name is Johnathan, and this is Isha, Michael, and Jeremy," replied Johnathan.

"So, what may I ask has brought you out here," said Timothy.

"We are just passing through," said Johnathan. "And you?"

"We too were trying to pass through as well, but we can't seem to find our way out of these woods. Just as it seems as though we are heading in the right direction, we end up right back here in the same place where we began. I am telling you, that you as well may not make it out either." Although Johnathan you do seem to be a man with much wisdom."

"Yes, I have some. God has sent me on a mission," said Johnathan "and he will show me where to go if he wishes for me to finish his plans for myself and my followers."

"I see," said Timothy. "Well, come and rest with us for now before you continue on your way."

The three men wanted to go with us or so they said but I didn't really trust them. I am pretty sure that none of the guys did either. But we did our best to help as God would want us to. Until we found out what they were, human clones, and then we could do no more for them.

These people had escaped from some kind of facility where they had been cloned. These people were not made by the hands of God but by another man's hand. This made them just as dangerous as the people with the mark. When looking at them you could tell that something wasn't right with them. They seemed more lost than we did. You could tell they had no soul.

"Yes, that's correct," said Timothy. "We were cloned in a facility down in Louisiana and we wish to join you on your journey. It has been so long since we have seen any other humans, and we could use your help to find civilization. We wouldn't be any bother, and in fact we may even be able to help you with the skills we have learned out here in the wild."

Johnathan tries to speak but Timothy cuts him off.

"Now, you don't have to give us an answer right now, just sleep on it and we will talk first thing in the morning."

All I kept thinking was, would we be safe here until morning?

"Okay," replied Johnathan. "I will do that, but first I must go off and pray to my Lord."

"Take all the time you need," replied Timothy.

Johnathan went off to speak with God. This was his daily routine. All Johnthan tells is that God had instructed us to get rid of them. They were going to cause more harm than good for us. Since we thought of them as not being real humans, choosing not to help them would not be a very difficult decision. Still the guys took care of the dirty work because they didn't want me to have to go through with something that might cause me any more stress. They were only trying to protect me. I am not exactly sure what they had said to them to get the men to follow them. They led the three men into the woods where they talked for a while. Then they were led deeper into the woods where I was unable to see what was going on. Then Johnathan, Jeremy, and Michael returned out of the woods about an hour later. They didn't want to tell me much, but I think the cloned people were later set on fire. As they slept in the woods for the night, a forest fire had broken out and we could see the flames in the distance as the day started to turn to night.

As I began to close my eyes to sleep for the night, I began to dream. In my dreams, I would see many faces of people that would appear to fade in and out of darkness. Coming closer to my face just to disappear back into the darkness again. I would look to the left and then to the right, but the faces seemed to come directly in front of me. Straight at my face then fade off as they almost touched my face. I didn't understand what was happening. It was scary because these were faces of people I had never seen in my whole life. The people weren't bothering me, but something didn't feel right, and I didn't understand what was happening. I jumped up from my sleep and took a quick look around. Johnathan, Michael, and Jeremy are fast asleep.

Whenever I close my eyes again, I would be back looking at these faces. Even before I had fallen asleep, they would appear as soon as my eye lids closed. I would open my eyes again to see the quiet night sky and the guys fast asleep. I laid there for a little while with my eyes open, but I was so tired I eventually fell back to sleep.

Entering again into a rem sleep state I began to have a second dream. I can feel a negative presence around me even before I see anything. I find myself walking down a sidewalk in a small town. I have my head down as I am looking at the sidewalks made of cobblestone.   I then look up and see a strange looking man with a top hat wearing a long tan trench coat. He just laughs at me as he walks by. I get the feeling that he somehow feels he has tricked me. He continued to stand behind me making me feel as if he could control my ways and thoughts. Speaking negative things into my ears to frighten me. Just before I woke, he spoke to me and said, "There is no one left but you. Your family is already gone. Come with me and I will take you to them." I began yelling in my dream for one of the guys to wake me up, but no one could hear me. I told the man I wasn't going with him and to leave me alone. While still in the dream I started to cry out to God in prayer asking him to wake me up. Just then my body is jolted again, and I jumped back out of the dream and with my heart racing I looked around again. What was happening to me? These nightmares seemed so real. I almost couldn't tell the dreams from reality.

By this time, I am really flipping out. I went and lay next to Michael for comfort but tried not to wake him. He rolls over and puts his arm around me and I lay on his chest. At this point, I couldn't go back to sleep. He asked me if everything was all right. I nodded yes and just laid there looking up into the dark sky waiting for the sun to rise again.

 As a new day began, with the wind blowing the leaves in the trees, I couldn't help but wonder what the day would bring that day.

In the next few weeks of our travel, I began to become weak in my mind. We had been walking for what seemed like an eternity, only stopping to eat, rest, and read "The Holy Bible." There was only one Bible for all of us to read since Bibles were no longer easy to come by. Every morning, we would read the Bible in the book of Revelation before we would begin walking. Revelation would tell us the next event that would take place on earth so we could be one step ahead.

As we walked through the woods, I began to look around. There didn't appear to be any signs of life. It appears many of the animals had moved on to find a safer place to live.

"Are we ever going to get out of these woods," I said. There were no real signs of life out here."

"You're right," said Michael. "Animals can always sense when bad things are going to happen like a built-in sensor that goes off and warns them to hide."

"We are beginning to run low on food, and I know that our faith was really being tested," I said.

Some people believe that God doesn't test you, but I always believed that in some ways he did. The guys were becoming restless, but Johnathan stood strong and continued to lead the group.

The weather wasn't too bad that day. The sun was lighting our way with a clear blue sky that surrounded us with no clouds nearby. Just up ahead, I could finally see a clearing. We were almost out of the woods. I thought this would make travel easy for us.

As we reached the edge of the forest, I looked out ahead at the land in front of us. It looked as though it was once someone's farmland.

You could still see some of the broken corn stalks sticking out from the ground. Once we got out a little from the woods, I began to look around again to see if there were any signs of people passing through the land. Yet once again there were no signs of life, and the large, deserted area didn't seem to lead anywhere. The sun began to beat directly down on us since there weren't any trees there to protect us from the direct sunlight. It seemed to be a little hotter outside now, but we had made it through worse days. I couldn't complain because at least there was a breeze. The calm wind was just enough to keep us moving. No one talked much that day as we walked because we all had to conserve our energy. That day was one of the last times that I looked up and enjoyed God's beauty of the world.   I could tell on that day; things were going to start looking up for us. We had read the next part of Revelation and understood what prophecy was going to be fulfilled next. Now it was just a matter of time until the next event would take place. But little did I know, we were about to have a little event of our own.

Just as I began to believe we were going to have a good day, it happened. Johnathan and Jeremy were walking just a few feet ahead of Michael and me. We could hear Jeremy starting to get upset with Johnathan. We didn't think much of it since we had seen them not get along before. That is just what brothers do.

Jeremy then began to question Johnathan's judgment.

"Do you even know if we are going in the right direction?" said Jeremy.

"You must be patient," replied Johnathan.

"We have been following you for days and haven't seen any food or people. We are beginning to run low on supplies and food. Are you sure that God is telling you to lead us this way? Maybe you are confused. Is God going to allow us to die out here?"

"Now you already know the answer to that question. God has a plan for us little brother, but you must be patient."

"Patient! Patient!! Have we not been patient? Have we not done all that you have asked of us Lord?" Jeremy looks up towards the sky.

"Now that's enough," said Johnathan in a stern voice. "Just stop. Don't say another word."

Johnathan reaches over to console his brother to let him know that it will be okay. Johnathan tries to put his hand on Jeremy's shoulder, but Jeremy knocks it off. Jeremy then continues to have a conversation with God.

"Did we not stand up against the anti-Christ and refused to take the mark of the beast? Now you leave us out here to die. Why? Why should we continue to worship you when you have forsaken us? What kind of God are you?"

Then Jeremy looks up into the sky and shouts out the name of another god that he says he will worship. Nothing happened. Johnathan again tries to get Jeremy to take a moment to calm down and help him to collect himself.

But then Jeremy stretched out his arms and says to God,

"I have all the power."

Just then dark clouds formed and came over us very quickly in just a matter of seconds. The sky had become as dark as night. It began to rain heavily. We all looked up to see what was going to happen next. It had almost looked like the clouds had divided the sky down the middle with an opening just above our heads. Just then there was a loud crackle of thunder and Jeremy dropped to the ground and fell on his knees. All at once he had become deathly ill.

Johnathan had run over to help him up from the ground, but there wasn't much he could do now. Jeremy thought he had more power than God and God punished him for trying to be king over him. No man shall ever be greater than his creator God. I came over to comfort Johnathan as he continued to try to help his brother up from the ground. Micheal was on his right side while I was on his left. Johnathan wanted us to help him carry Jeremy, but it was impossible because we would barely carry ourselves. Besides, he had made God mad, and Michael and I didn't want to do the same. Jeremy made a choice, one that destroyed his life.

"I'm sorry," I told Johnathan, "But you are going to have to let him go."

His brother lay there in his arms shaking and very weak with pneumonia. Johnathan just cried out in a loud voice.

"No!"

He tried to carry Jeremy for a while. I told him that he was dead.

Johnathan replied, "But he's, my brother."

"I know," I told him. "But his spirit is gone, and he is no longer a man of God, so he is no good to us now.

I grabbed his arm and told him that it was time to go. Michael then grabbed his other arm to make sure he would not return. Jeremy laid there in the rain to die.

Johnathan didn't want to leave his brother, but God was angry, and Michael and I knew that there was nothing more that we could do to help Jeremy. We loved Jeremy very much but our love for God was much stronger. We could only do what he wanted us to do. We did our best to help Johnathan make it through the day, but you could tell that he had suffered a great loss when he lost his brother.

That evening while resting around the campfire Michael and Johnathan had a long chat that night. I pretended to sleep to give them some time to talk. I listened carefully as Johnathan had begun to blame himself.

"It is all my fault," cried Johnathan. "I should have taught him more about the Lord. If I could have only stopped him from speaking those words unto the Lord, this wouldn't have happened."

"It's not your fault," replied Michael. "Your brother made a choice not to obey God. You were not responsible for his choices. It was up to Jeremy to seek and understand God for himself. You guided him in the best way you knew how, but he didn't put in enough effort on his end."

"Michael, I know you are completely right, but it is just so hard for me to take it all in right now. Thank you for talking with me, but now I must go out and pray to the Lord. Get some sleep and I shall return before morning."

"Okay but be careful. I will be looking for you in the morning if you are not back here."

"Okay."

"Isha, you can get up now," said Michael.

"I am really worried about him," I replied. "You don't think he will do anything crazy tonight?"

"No, I just think he needs a little bit of time."

The next morning, we had awoken earlier than normal since Michael, and I were worried about Johnathan. We really couldn't sleep either after a day like yesterday. We had just enough food to last us one more day, and then we would really have to start looking for food.

"Johnathan come and join us for breakfast," I replied.

"No thank you. I really am not that hungry," he answered.

"Look Johnathan, we still need you so please come and eat so that you will have some energy."

Johnathan came over after talking to him for a few minutes. Michael and I were glad because we knew that we needed him to guide us. God spoke to him the strongest and he always knew which way that God wanted us to go.

"Why has he chosen me to lead when I don't seem to be getting anywhere?" asked Johnathan. "And why was it that when I tried to speak with him last night, I received no answer?"

"Maybe you already knew the answer to the question that you were asking," said Michael. "Look, I know it has been hard on all of us, but we must put everything aside because we know that God has something better for us if we continue to do his will, so let's just move on until he tells us when it's time to stop."

"I agree," I said. "You have been doing a great job and we will continue to take it one day at a time."

We kept walking quietly to conserve our energy. We passed one broken corn stalk after another. There really wasn't much else to look at. After walking about five miles out from where we had started this morning we decided to stop and take a ten-minute rest. Just then we all looked up and spotted what appeared to be a small house. We had only been walking for about an hour and it was just now about 8:00am. Not sure what we would find there, but a little bit of excitement filled our spirits. So, we eagerly decided to stop at the house for a break. Johnathan had a smile on his face, for he was pleased.

"What do you think we will find there?" said Isha.

"I am sure that we will be able to find anything left behind by the people who left," said Johnathan. "Maybe some canned food."

"I know I am getting my hopes up, but it sure would be nice to have some pineapple," said Michael. "I haven't had pineapple in such a long time, and it is my absolute favorite fruit.

"We know," said Johnathan and Isha. We had only heard him say that about a hundred times before.

"Well, at least we will have some kind of shelter for the night," said Johnathan.

As we got closer to the little house, we realized it wasn't as little as we thought. We came up facing the back of the house and at first glance it didn't appear to have any residents inside. The house was an all-brick house that had been painted sky blue. There were two smaller windows at the back of the house and between them was the back door. We could smell something coming from the house. Johnathan gently knocks on the door. A woman wrapped in a red gown answers the door and with no hesitation invites us in. Her hair was also in a wrap, but her face was completely uncovered. She was Arabic as were the other three women who dressed in the same manor.

Johnathan says, "good morning."

The woman at the door just nodded her head. Then the women began to retrieve dry clothes for us. They happily welcomed us into their home to bathe and clean up. While we were all getting comfortable and dry the scent, we smelled only grew stronger. Whatever they were cooking smelled rather good. The head woman of the household did not speak a work to us as if she wanted to make sure we were comfortable first. Once everyone was all washed up, we gathered back into the living room. Johnathan began to speak to the woman again. He thanked the women for all their help and asked them why they were unafraid when we came to their door.

"My name is Rahab," she replied. "God told us you were coming. We have been waiting for your arrival. God instructed us on what we would need to set aside for your arrival this day. We made sure we had clean clothes for all to wear and a warm meal for all to eat. God speaks to me the same way that he speaks to you Johnathan, and I can tell that he is very proud of you. You are a very strong-minded man so don't let anyone distract you from following God."

"Thank you very much," replied Johnathan. "Are you sure that you have enough for us to join you in this meal?"

"I have already told you that God has made enough for all, but after we eat you must rest. God wants you to rest for forty-eight hours before returning on your journey. So please if you need anything while you are here do not hesitate to ask. When your time is up, I will guide you to the best way to reach your destination.

Sitting on the couch I had some time to reflect. I began started thinking about how God works. Remembering how dreadful things happen and they seem to all happen at once. For instance, your car breaks down and you don't have enough money to repair it. Therefore, you must find a ride to work. Then the person giving you a ride becomes unreliable, so you end up losing your job. Losing your job now means you won't have enough money to pay your rent for the next month. Bad things come in showers. First, it's a little drizzle then it becomes a down pour. Then from the hard downpour it turns into a flood. It's just funny how God always comes before the water gets too high that you can't get out. But God saves you and you become over filled with joy. The water may come up to your neck, but he saves you just before your head goes under. He gives you more than you have asked for, but he gives you all that you need. God's love and logic is greater than any man. Sitting back on the couch looking up at the ceiling I began remembering what miracles God did for me.

The very first time that I really remember him being there with me was when I was seven. I was outside of my aunt's house on the sidewalk just below the steps that led to the front door. I was trying to teach myself how to pop a wheelie on my bike. I didn't know what I was doing but I had watched my brother and cousins do it all the time. I was the youngest of them all and so I was really determined to learn something that they all knew how to do. So, I kept trying but all I could do was a small jump called a bunny hop. I finally got the bike up high enough, but it went a little too high and then the bike came down on me. I hit the back of my head on the concrete and with the impact of the fall I should have felt some pain. I heard the noise of my head hitting the concrete, but I felt nothing. It was like I had just laid back onto a soft pillow. I quickly jumped up scared but without a scratch or knot on my head. I quickly thanked Jesus and ran into the house. I was done trying to learn how to do a wheelie.

"So, what's the game plan?" I asked Johnathan.

"Well, I suggest you two get a good night's sleep because we will be heading out after breakfast in the morning," said Johnathan.

"I was really beginning to enjoy those soft comfortable beds," said Michael. "It was so much softer than the ground. I am going to bed early so that I can enjoy that bed for a little while longer while I have the chance."

"I know things haven't been easy for us, but I am really glad that you guys stood by me and believed in me," said Johnathan. "That really means a lot to me."

"No problem," said Michael. "I know you will take us to where we would need to be."

These last couple of days had really made a difference in Johnathan's behavior. He still has his quiet moments where you can tell he still thinks of his brother, but now he is more determined than before to finish what God has led him to do. We have done everything to lift his spirits and to encourage him to keep listening to God.

Chapter 3

<u>A New Day</u>

A new day begins.

Following a new passage

The message comes fast.

So do not look passed it.

Follow the signs.

They lead you not a stray.

You will have what you need.

Until that glorious day.

"So, what's the game plan?" I asked Johnathan.

"Well, I suggest you two get a good night's sleep because we will be heading out after breakfast in the morning.

"I was really beginning to enjoy those soft comfortable beds," said Michael. "It was so much softer than the ground. I'm going to bed early, so I can enjoy having a bed for a little while longer while I have the chance."

"I know things haven't been easy for us, but I am really glad that you guys stood by me and believed in me," said Johnathan. "That really means a lot to me."

"No problem. I knew you would take us to where we would need to be," said Michael.

These last few days have really made a significant difference in Johnathan's behavior. He still has his quiet moments where you can tell he still thinks of his brother, but now he is more determined than before to finish what God has led him to do. We have done everything to lift his spirits and to encourage him to keep listening to God.

We began on our way again praying many blessings to fall on the 4 women who have taken care of us for the last couple of days. And they too blessed us on our journey to God. They gave us gold treasures to trade with anyone who would accept them as payment for food or necessities that we would need.

This time we only had to walk a day and a half to see some kind of civilization. We had made it through the forest and then through the plains, and now we were in some small city.

As we approached the city, we could see the sight of modern skyscrapers as well as some smaller historical buildings. The city is nestled in a valley, surrounded by gently rolling hills with emerald, green grass and colorful wildflowers swaying in the breeze. The streets were filled with activity, as the people went about their daily routines. Market stalls line the cobblestone streets, offering an array of goods ranging from fresh produce to handcrafted wares. A majestic fountain stands at its center with its waters sparkling in the sunlight. Surrounding the square city are quaint shops and cafes, with colorful banners and flower boxes overflowing with blooms.

The people of the city were living with the mark of the beast which meant that we would most likely not be able to buy any food. The city gave me a weird feeling. It was almost like everyone was a robot or some kind of zombie. You could clearly see that we did not blend in with any of the people that surrounded us. No one seemed to be in a rush to go anywhere, and so it just seemed as though they were doing things just to be doing something. It was like they didn't have an actual brain of their own. If I had ever felt that I was different, then today topped all the other days. No one seemed to even care that we were here.

After walking around for a few minutes, we started to get hungry while smelling the aroma of fresh hamburgers cooking in a café nearby. I told them that I wanted to rest, so I sat on a bench just outside the marketplace.

The two guys went on walking to try to trade some of the gold for some supplies. While they were gone a nice-looking gentleman walked by me and into the market. He was staring extremely hard, and then he smiled as he continued into the store. I sat there wondering what he was thinking. I wasn't sure if that was a smile of pity or a smile of laughter to make fun of someone less fortunate or what.

Although he wasn't in my sight for more than a few seconds I could remember exactly what he looked like. He had short brown hair and brown eyes. The mark was located on his forehead. The man wore a blue suit with black shiny shoes. He had a tan complexion, but I was unable to figure out what nationality he could be. He was not bad looking, but not my type by any means. Anyone who could sell their soul is far from gaining my heart.

Well, about 15 minutes later he returns from out of the store with about six grocery bags. Now this time he stops beside the bench and says hi. I said hi in return just wondering what he was up to. He leans over and hands me 2 brown paper bags full of groceries.

He speaks in a soft voice. "I think these might help you along your journey."

I thanked him greatly and he began on down the street. I was truly shocked by what had just happened. Not knowing what else to do but thank God.

"Thank you, God."

God is truly amazing the way he can touch the heart of anyone good or bad just to bless you. God works through all kinds of people and for that reason it is always best to be nice to one another because you never know when you or they might need help.

I quickly began to look for Johnathan and Michael. I walked about 2 blocks down when I saw them coming out of a quick stop gas station store.

"Look what I've got!" I yelled.

"Isha, how did you get all of these things," asked Johnathan.

"A nice gentleman gave them to me at the supermarket a couple of blocks back."

"What did you give to him in return?"

"Nothing."

"Was he a man of God?"

"No."

"Then how can we trust this food is good?"

"They are all things that are sealed except the bag of apples.

"And why do you think he would just give you all of these things without paying for them one way or another," said Michael.

"I'm not sure. I just knew that God had sent the man to us when he said that he knew these things would help us along our journey. And he spoke in a soft voice the way that God often sounds when he speaks to me. I mean, after all, we must bless our food anyway."

"She's right," replied Johnathan. "We will bless it up to God and we shall all be okay. Now let's all take a moment to give thanks to God for another wonderful blessing."

Johnathan begins to pray aloud.

"God, we have come in your name to give thanks for all that you do. And we especially want to thank you for the food you have so graciously given unto us. Bless it all and allow it to nourish our bodies and give us strength to make it to our destination. Continue to watch over us as we travel and allow no illness or sickness to fall upon us. Continue to show us the right path that will lead us to our home in heaven. And most importantly allow our minds to stay strong and focused on our goal. Do not allow us to fall astray from the pack but allow us to work together at all times. Father, forgive us for our sins as we do try not to sin. Forgive the ones who have tried to bring sin against us to defeat our cause. We pray all these things in the mighty name of Jesus, and we all said Amen."

As we continued to walk that day, we had a little more pep in our steps because God had truly lifted our spirits with joy once again. He just never stops amazing us with his presence ever so near that keeps us safe. In my eyes God has never been cross but don't ever cross him and he won't have to be. God has so much love inside that he wants to share with the world.

On one of our breaks Johnathan goes away from us to pray. He is gone for about an hour. While he is away, he begins to have a premonition. This premonition stays in Johnathan's mind. This premonition came to him much stronger than any others. Johnathan tells us that he was sleeping in his vision and when he awoke there was a lot of water. Johnathan sees more but doesn't want to alarm us. Then God reassures him that everything will be okay and that his path will only lead them to happiness and eternal life with God.

So, the next day we ended up on a boat to Hawaii. And I admit, Michael and I were a little worried to see how this day would turn out. It was a pretty large boat but not quite as big as one of those cruise boats. This one was like a mini cruise boat. It was all white with blue trim on the bottom. The name of the boat was called, "The Blue Treasure."

The letters were spelled out in blue with cursive letters.

Once again no one bothered us, or even seemed to notice us for that matter. Everyone was too busy enjoying the sun and their cocktail drinks. Everyone was enjoying themselves with gourmet food, dancing, and site sightseeing. Yet somehow still remarkably similar to the people of the small town, zombie like but not as much as before. I must admit it seemed kind of peaceful and the weather was really good for traveling. I felt at ease.

Standing beside Micheal while looking out over the water as we traveled across the waves. I glanced over at Michael who was in deep thought.

"What are you thinking about," I asked Michael.

"Just how God can still create such beautiful days in the midst of all the sadness, replied Michael. "Don't you think today is a nice day, Isha?"

"Absolutely," I replied.

I wanted to say, so aren't you worried about Johnathan's premonition? I didn't want to bring it up since he too was having a good day. Although, I was a little nervous about how the day might end. I decided to put it out of my mind as Michael had done. So, I wrapped my arm around his, laid my head on his shoulder, while looking out into the water. Feeling the cool breeze running through our hair and the fresh air in our faces.

When we finally arrived, we set up camp near one of the beach shorelines where we had stayed for two nights. I enjoyed it very much as far as the beauty and the weather went but I sure did miss those comfortable beds at Rahab's place. I couldn't complain though since we had made it to Hawaii safely. I'd say that I have seen more of the world with these men than I would have ever had the chance to do if I had never met them. We had most definitely been on a long journey. Of course, it will be well worth the wait when our heavenly father rewards us with a place near him in his divine kingdom in heaven.

At the end of our second night, we did our usual prayers and praises to God and things seem to become a little easier for us, at least in our minds. Sometimes, I would still think of Jeremy and some of the funny things he would say if he were around. He would always say, "Come on Isha you know that was funny." Then I would try my hardest not to laugh at his corny jokes. They were so silly that you had to laugh.

Michael had been out on a morning walk during our second week and third day on the beach when he had overheard some people talking about an intense storm coming through. It was supposed to start around midnight and go on into the early morning hours.

"Oh great," I said. "Just what we need, considering that we really don't have any shelter right now. All we have is this tent and that won't hold up to any substantial amounts of wind."

"What are we going to do now," asked Michael.

"Well, God tells me to wait," said Johnathan.

"Wait! where?" Michael said excitedly.

"Right here at the coastline."

"Why would we want to do that?"

"Look," says Johnathan. "When the snack stand closes down for the night, we will take shelter in there, but we are not to leave this area. Is that okay with you guys?"

"I don't think that little stand is going to do us any good," said Michael. "We might as well stay out here in the tent all night."

 "Well, we should be just fine since it will only be for one night.

"We both nodded yes in agreement although we really didn't agree.

"Then it is settled," says Johnathan. "God has instructed us to stay near the shorelines, and so until he tells us to move, we will obey."

This must have been Johnathan's entire premonition, and here I thought it had something to do with the boat ride across into Hawaii.

We sat down around 8:00pm and ate. Then we prayed for about an hour straight. Prayer was especially important to us for our survival in this world and especially now more than ever. We finally got to sleep in the snack shack at around 10pm. Although none of us carried a watch or clock, Johnathan could tell us what time of the day it was. And about nine times out of ten he would be right. Michael and I tried, but we were more like a 4 or 6 out of ten. I guess boy scouts did teach him a few good lessons for survival.

It was about daybreak when we were awakened by the snack shack shaking. At first Michael and I thought it was some kids outside playing. We thought they were trying to scare us by rocking the shack back and forth. After it stopped about 3 minutes later, we got up to look around and see what was going on. Not sure what we would find, we held onto one another tight. It wasn't raining and there weren't any dark clouds in the sky. Just then we heard people screaming and the earth shook again.

"An earthquake!" I shouted.

There weren't earthquakes in Hawaii, but this was an earthquake. Thousands of people were running from the city to the shore to escape the earthquake. People started heading for the emergency boats by the shoreline that they used when a volcano was going to erupt. Johnathan led us down to boat # 5 where we sat until it was filled with about 6 more people. One young man named Jeremiah knew how to drive the boat and so once everyone was inside, he headed out away from the island.

We began to see many people that we knew and hadn't seen for a while until today. We saw old friends and coworkers that were running for safety as the earth did not stop shaking. We got out in the water about 5 minutes from the shore and you could see people dying while others were trying to swim to safety, but the main island Honolulu of Hawaii was done with. The land had broken so much it was no longer an island. The water started getting very rocky, and I was praying we would be okay. The earthquake had now become a tsunami.

Once we got over a rough patch, I could see the waves beginning to divide the land farther apart. We had finally made it to another island safely as the waves had pushed us the way we needed to go. God had put his people on one island and all the others you could hear crying out for us to come back and get them. I felt incredibly sad that I was unable to help those people in need, but they had not listened to God and were therefore punished. The water was almost like an invisible wall, or whirlpool that had kept them on one side unable to make it to safety. God did not want us to go back for them. After all of God's people were safe the water became way too rough. I felt like I was already in heaven looking down and seeing the people in hell. From there, we ascended to heaven never to look back upon the earth again. God had allowed us to make it to his promised land. He had kept his word. He shall endure forever. Let no man cross his path. Let your faith make you whole. May your strength come from above. Amen.